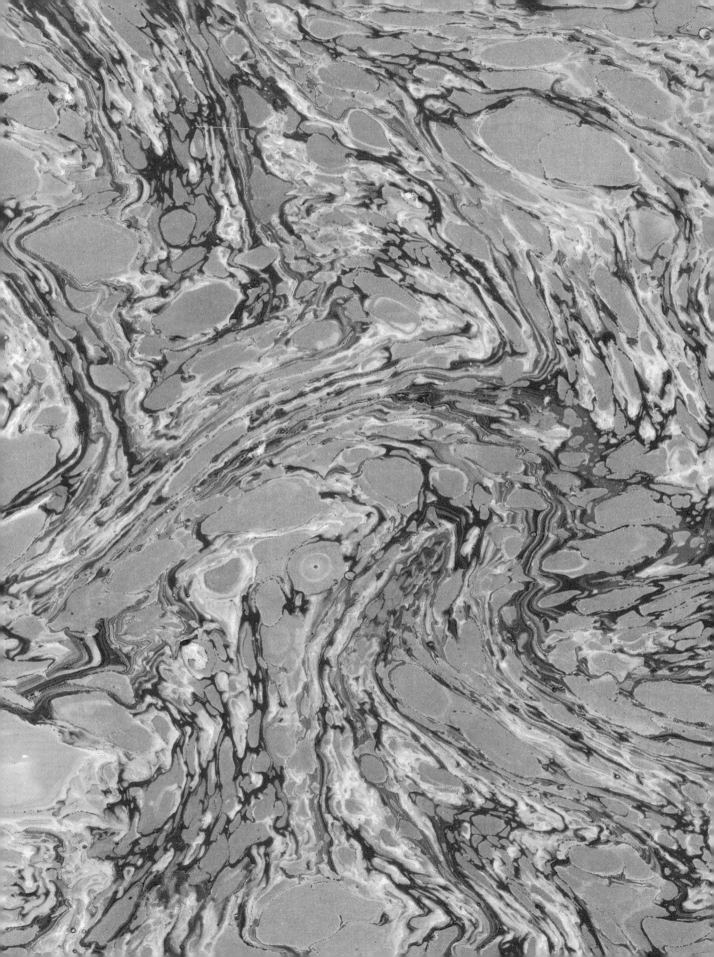

CHARLES PERRAULT

Cinderella

RETOLD BY CHRISTINE SAN JOSÉ

ILLUSTRATED BY DEBRAH SANTINI

BOYDS MILLS PRESS

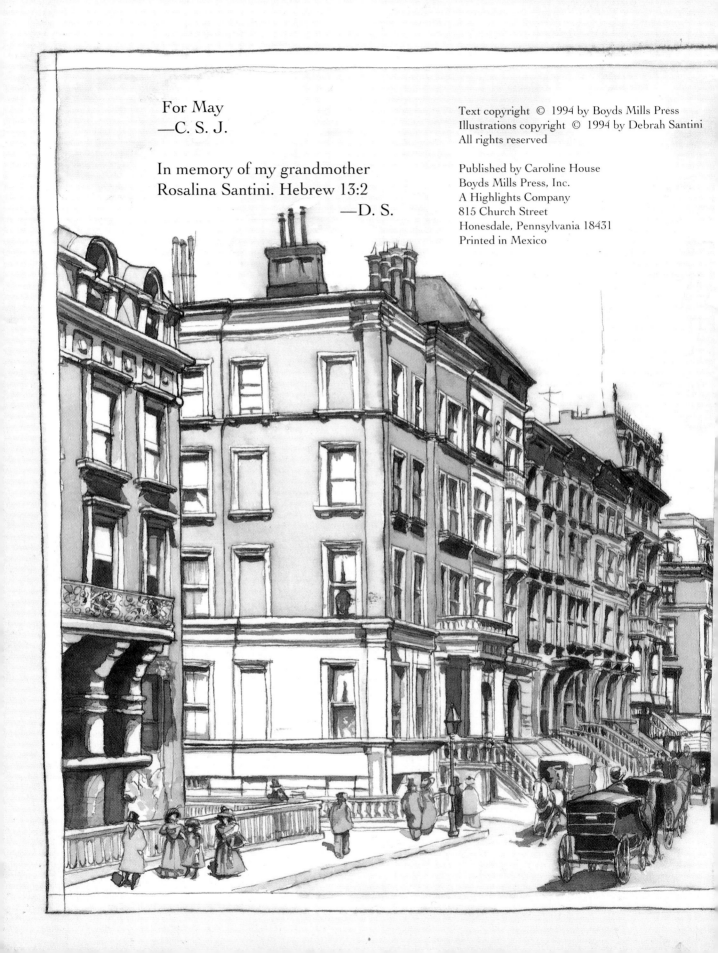

For May
—C. S. J.

In memory of my grandmother
Rosalina Santini. Hebrew 13:2
—D. S.

Text copyright © 1994 by Boyds Mills Press
Illustrations copyright © 1994 by Debrah Santini

Published by Caroline House
Boyds Mills Press, Inc.
A Highlights Company
815 Church Street
Honesdale, Pennsylvania 18431
Printed in Mexico

Publisher Cataloging-in-Publication Data
Perrault, Charles.
  Cinderella / Charles Perrault ; retold by
Christine San José ;
illustrated by Debrah Santini. — 1st ed.
[32]p. : col. ill. ; cm.
Summary : A modern adaptation of the classic fairy tale
by Charles Perrault.
ISBN 1-56397-152-6
[1. Fairy tales. 2. Princesses — Fiction.]
I. Perrault, Charles. II. San José, Christine, reteller.
III. Santini, Debrah, ill. IV. Title.
  [E] — dc20   1994
Library of Congress Catalog Card Number 92-73991   CIP

First edition, 1994
Book designed by Tim Gillner
The text of this book is set in 16-point Cochin.
The illustrations are done in watercolor.
Distributed by St. Martin's Press

10 9 8 7 6 5 4 3 2

There was once a kind and beautiful girl who lived happily with her kind and beautiful mama and her wealthy papa. But alas her mama died. And her papa married again.

Her stepmother was a widow with two daughters of her own. The girl welcomed them to the house. But for all her good will toward them, she had to see that they were more vain, more selfish, and more ill-natured than she could ever have imagined.

"That wretched girl!" she heard her stepmother say to her own daughters. "She makes herself seem so much better than you two, my dears."

And to make sure no one should see how kind and beautiful the girl was, the stepmother and her daughters tired her out all day with the grimiest of household chores. At night they banished her to the attic, to a stained old mattress leaking moldy straw.

The girl knew nothing would come of troubling her father. He was rarely at home. He was busy making money for his extravagant new wife, who had him completely under her thumb. The only comfort for the girl was a little warmth at night from the kitchen hearth. Before her climb to the freezing attic, she would sit a while, exhausted, among the cinders.

Once, her stepsisters saw her and jeered, "Cinderella! Let's call her Cinderella! Our Princess of the Cinders!"

So Cinderella she became. And truth to tell, though her stepsisters flaunted velvet while she wore rags, she was more the princess than they. For she never quite lost her cheerful grace.

N ow came a great stir. The Prince was planning a ball, and he sent a splendid invitation to every important family, including Cinderella's. The stepsisters were so excited they tore the invitation from each other's hands. (Cinderella had to piece it back together.) They called in dressmakers and shoemakers and milliners. (Cinderella had to stitch on a hundred extra frills, and pleat and starch and iron.) They paraded endlessly in front of their full-length mirrors. (Cinderella had to hold up looking glasses in both hands so they could see themselves front and back and both sides.) They starved themselves to fit into their wasp-waisted creations. (But when the great day came, Cinderella still had to tug on their corset laces for all she was worth, and three of them broke as the sisters screamed "Tighter! Tighter!")

At last they preened in their perfection, painted and powdered and primped to the nines.

"Sweet Princess of the Cinders," they purred, "why aren't you preparing your *toilette*? How could there be a royal ball without you?"

And so with cruel banter they pranced into the family carriage with their mother and rode away.

Cinderella sank among the cinders. She longed to go to the ball. But she brushed away a tear that started. She tried to hum a little waltz that her mother had taught her. She tried to dance a step or two.

"Why don't you go?"

Cinderella spun around. Who was that? The voice came from the shadows by the chimney corner. And standing there was an elegant woman with shining eyes.

"Come, girl," the woman said. "There's no time to lose. Fairy godmothers help those who help themselves. Bring the biggest pumpkin you can find to the kitchen door." Astonished but on flying feet, Cinderella brought the pumpkin.

"Scoop it out!"

In a trice Cinderella had scooped it to the rind. Her god-mother barely touched it with her cane, and before them glowed a magnificent golden coach.

"Now four live mice from the mousetraps! Hurry!"

Cinderella happily set the little creatures free. She clapped her hands in delight as her godmother turned them into four fine white horses.

"Hmm," now said the fairy godmother. "We need a coachman."

Spying a plump, long-whiskered rat in the rattrap, Cinderella touched him to her godmother's cane, and he was a roly-poly coachman twirling his moustache.

"Six lizards from behind the water butt!" came the godmother's final command. And Cinderella had six footmen in gleaming green livery to attend her.

She had quite forgotten she was in rags. But now she looked hesitantly at her fairy godmother.

"Well, well, then, girl, there you go," said the woman. And touching her goddaughter with her cane, she left her radiant in white silk and tiny seed pearls, a diadem on her head, and on her feet a pair of sparkling glass slippers.

"How can I ever thank you, Godmama?" asked Cinderella as she climbed into the golden coach.

"Just be yourself, dear," said her godmother, closing the coach door for her. "And be sure you're back before the clock strikes twelve. Because that's when your coach and your horses and your coachman and your footmen and your gown and all your fine jewels turn back into what they were.

Remember, before the clock strikes twelve." With that the fairy godmother signaled the coachman to crack his whip, and off went Cinderella to the ball.

Cinderella looked out her golden windows at the blue night rushing by. Lanterns hung everywhere to light the way to the palace. And was it really she outlined in the glass, with a diamond circlet in her hair?

She rode through the palace gates, and the horses' hooves clattered across the courtyard. The massive palace doors stood wide, and she heard music and laughter. A handsome, grave young man opened the golden coach door and helped her alight. It was the Prince himself, come to greet so illustrious a guest. She went into the palace on his arm.

$\mathbf{A}$s he led her down the staircase to the ballroom, all eyes were on Cinderella's loveliness. The talkers fell silent, and the musicians forgot to play. Then "Who is she? Who can she be?" they began to whisper.

The orchestra struck up a waltz. And as Cinderella and the Prince led the dance, everyone marveled at the airy spirit of her step and the elegant flow of her gown, but above all at the glowing kindness in her smile.

Cinderella and the Prince found a hundred things to talk about. He had eyes and ears for no one but her, and she knew he was the friend she had looked for all her life. When the feast was spread, he piled her plate with special delicacies: purple figs from the princely fig tree, cherry tartlets baked by his old nurse.

Cinderella sought her stepmother and stepsisters to share them because she was good-hearted, and just a little, truth to tell, because it was fun to see their surprise at being singled out. For they had no idea who she was. They could not possibly see that the beautiful princess was their kitchen maid.

Time flew so fast that Cinderella thought the clock in the dining room must be wrong to chime half past eleven. But the ballroom clock answered the same. So she slipped away to her golden coach and rode home.

In the chimney corner, she found her godmother eager for her tale. Cinderella showed how she had twirled in the Prince's arms. But at that very moment the cuckoo in the old clock told midnight—and Cinderella was twirling barefoot in her rags!

Outside she heard four mice, six lizards, and a plump, long-whiskered rat skitter to their homes. Now voices came from the front entrance.

"My dears, her *style*!" the older daughter was saying. "Brilliant, but not gaudy. Quite simple, but never dull. Who can she be? The Prince told me she was from a foreign country."

"Liar!" said the younger. "He never spoke to you. She herself told me—"

"Oh, what did she say?" asked Cinderella, coming out from the kitchen, rubbing her eyes as if she'd been asleep.

"Keep your sooty nose out of the business of your betters, miss," snapped the younger sister. "Get up to the attic!"

Climbing the stairs, Cinderella heard her stepmother say, "Believe me, he'll never rest till he finds out who she is."

But how could she tell him? She was only the Princess of the Cinders. He might even think she had tricked him, pretending to be what she was not.

She tossed and turned till near dawn. Then in a dream of the enchanted ball, she heard the herald's trumpet blow—but no, it wasn't in her dream! She ran to the attic window. Down in the street the herald read his proclamation. This very night, at the palace, there would be another ball, just like the one the night before. And the Prince begged that every one of his guests would attend. Every one. And a third time the herald said it: Every one.

Cinderella was distraught: What should she do? But she was thrust into working her own magic with needle and thread for her stepmother and stepsisters frantic to be even grander than before. At last, as she curled the final topknot, she thought she heard her god-mother say, "You shall go." And as her stepsisters and their mother sailed splendiferously out the door, she knew she would see the Prince again and tell him.

Her fairy godmother was ready for her in the kitchen.

"Fresh pumpkin," the godmother said, "scooped. Four mice. Rat. Six lizards."

In no time Cinderella was in her coach, shimmering in cloth of silver, in her hair a sapphire deep as midnight, and on her feet the sparkling glass slippers.

"Home by twelve," her godmother reminded her, and Cinderella was on her way.

Past the lanterns, through the palace gates, the Prince there to meet her, to greet her, to dance with her, to talk. Tonight she would tell him. Later.

But time had wings. Too soon the clock was striking eleven.... No! It was twelve!

Cinderella fled from the ballroom. As she reached the courtyard, she lost one of her glass slippers. She snatched off the other and put it in her pocket. Now her silver gown was turned to rags. No coach. No horses. She threaded her way through the black alleyways so that no one should see her, and didn't rest till she sank among the cinders at home.

Almost at once it seemed she heard her stepmother and step-sisters return, exclaiming among themselves.

"Well, you couldn't expect him to go on with the festivities once she'd left!"

"—once she'd *vanished*, you mean! No princess, the gate guard said. No coach. Just a ragged girl slipping into the shadows . . ."

"And the glass slipper!"

"He says he'll search and search till he finds the owner. And she will be his bride."

Cinderella crept up to the attic. Oh, if only she could tell him! But then he would lose his dream entirely. He would know his princess was an illusion. As long as she kept hidden, he could always hope that one day, one day, he would find his true princess.

Before daybreak, heralds proclaimed officially the Prince's search for the owner of the glass slipper.

The slipper was carried far and wide so that everywhere young ladies of wealth or high degree, or both, were trying it on. But their feet were too long, or too short, or too wide, or too narrow, or their arches too high, or too low. The Prince was reported pale, thin, falling into a decline.

He took to riding with the slipper himself, to make sure that not one corner was overlooked.

So it happened that one morning two equerries and indeed the Prince pulled up outside Cinderella's home. In the drawing room, the older sister crammed her sausage-fat toes into the dainty slipper, but when she stood she couldn't hold back a shriek of pain. Then the younger sister forced in her angular heel, but when she tried to stand she fell right over.

Sadder than ever, the Prince was leaving when he caught sight of a face at the window.

"There is someone else to try the slipper!" he cried.

"But that's only the kitchen maid!" protested the stepmother and her daughters. "That's only Cinderella, Princess of the Cinders!"

The Prince was at the kitchen door. And the moment he saw Cinderella barefoot in her rags, grime beneath her fingernails—he knew she was his princess.

He offered her the glass slipper. From her pocket, Cinderella pulled its mate. She put the slippers on and for those who could hear it a little old waltz tune hung in the air. So they waltzed together, Cinderella and the Prince.

Soon after, they were married. The stepmother and her daughters, truth to tell, were still vain and selfish and ill-natured. But at least they were civil to Cinderella, to her face.

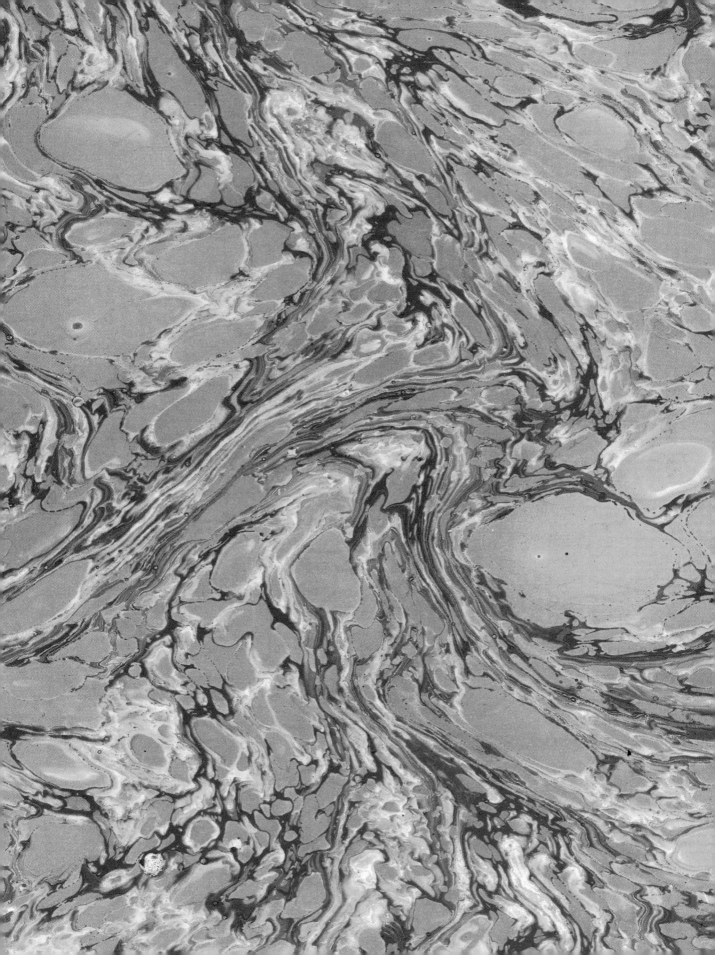

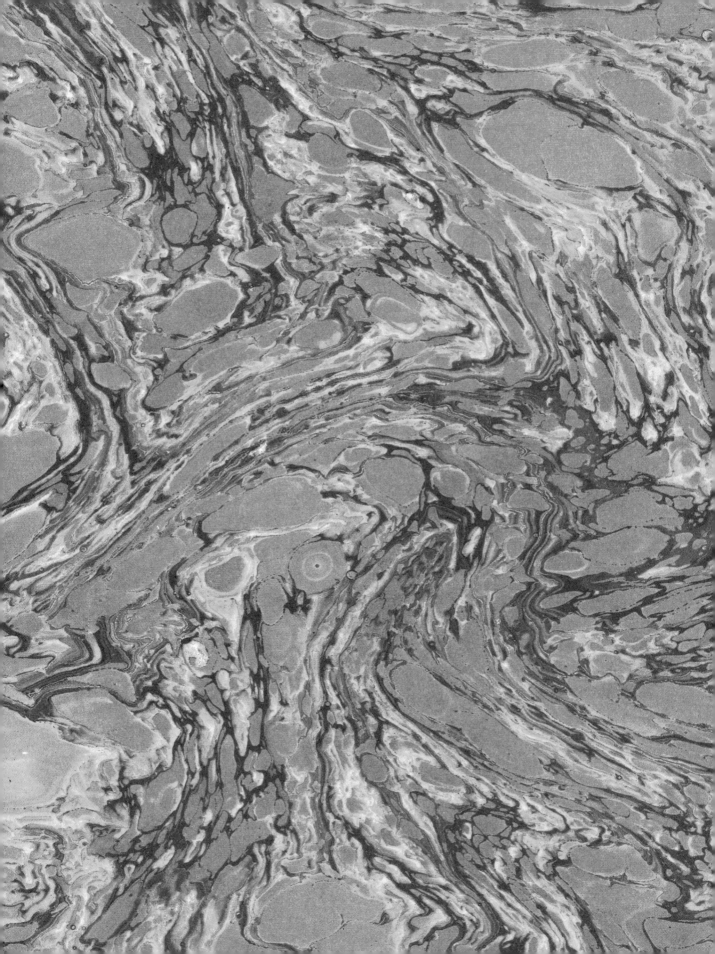